ANNIHILATION SONGS

THREE SHAKESPEARE REINTEGRATIONS

ACKNOWLEDGMENTS

These *Three Shakespeare Reintegrations* have appeared in various journal markets worldwide:

"Here Swims a Most Majestic Vision" appeared in *Rampike* (Canada), *The Barcelona Review*, *JAAM* (NZ), and online in *Exquisite Corpse* and elsewhere.

"The Execution of the Sun" appeared in *The Wisconsin Review*, *JAAM* (NZ), *The Abiko Quarterly* (Japan), and online in *Exquisite Corpse*, *Eclectica*, and elsewhere.

"Puzzles of War" first appeared in *Stand* (UK), *Landfall* (NZ), *Verandah* (Australia), and online in *The God Particle* (US).

Stalking Horse Press
Santa Fe, New Mexico

ANNIHILATION SONGS

Copyright © 2016 by Jason DeBoer
ISBN: 978-0-9970629-1-5
Library of Congress Control Number: 2016948088

First paperback edition published by Stalking Horse Press, December 2016

www.stalkinghorsepress.com

Design by James Reich
The Kiss by Edvard Munch, 1897

Stalking Horse Press
Santa Fe, New Mexico

Stalking Horse Press requests that authors designate a nonprofit, charitable, or humanitarian organization to receive a portion of revenue from the sales of each title. Jason DeBoer has chosen Esperanza Shelter for Battered Families, Inc. www.esperanzashelter.org

ANNIHILATION SONGS

INTRODUCTION

TOSH BERMAN

William Shakespeare wrote works of pleasure and intrigue. He had his fingers on the pulse of the ills of the world, as well as its gratification. The sensual and the horrific are often contained in one body. Jason DeBoer, with the spirit of Shakespeare looking over his shoulder, conveys the sense of dread, as well as its joy, in his three narratives in this book of "Shakespeare reintegrations," *Annihilation Songs.*

Like a skilled surgeon, DeBoer takes apart the texts of *The Tempest, The Two Gentlemen of Verona,* and *Hamlet.* The cut-ups can work as a sound piece, or a disorientated version of the original texts, but DeBoer, in his fresh way, makes new narrations, while still respecting the source material. One can explore the world in its own fashion with the Shakespeare plays, and the author here, takes the language and with a map of his own making, goes on a journey. He uses Shakespeare's plays as a map, but not as a destination from point A to get to point B.

Using existing language as the source material is a fine art and tradition. Dadaist Tristan Tzara did it with his poetry. William Burroughs did it with his fiction, and the Oulipo just did it as if they were a cat cornering a mouse in a room. DeBoer uses Shakespearean text, not only for the beauty of its language but also for divining new aesthetic possibilities. To appreciate and enjoy the DeBoer stories here, you don't have to read the original Shakespeare plays. They could be the additional texture, if one chooses to go that route. Meditations on war, love, sex, and power can be played out in numerous ways. I read the three stories straight through, not giving a thought to Shakespeare. The language and phrasing are familiar, but it is like a relative visiting you, and you don't know this person that well—yet, one feels a strong physical interconnection between the relative and the other family member. Art works in that fashion as well.

"Puzzles of War" is a reintegration of *Hamlet.* It opens with the brutal burial of soldiers during World War II, after the D-Day invasion. Cornelius, the hero of the story, runs amok from Sergeant Laertes and comes to meet a pregnant Gertrude, who is looking over the dead body of her husband. War has always been displayed as either a farce or a tragedy. "Puzzles of War" is both, due to the playfulness and usage of the language, and the very bona fide characters in the tale. *Hamlet* is such an iconic narrative, that perhaps the only way to give it praise is to actually use its language to reformat a new narrative. Boris Vian, a writer that I published with my press, TamTam Books, also played with history and classical literature to make fresh approaches to narratives. DeBoer, like Vian, is a bartender, who is not afraid to mix strange exotic liquids to make that perfect cocktail.

It has been reported by scholars that *The Tempest* was Shakespeare's last play. If that is true, it seems almost like a reflection of his past work in that he acknowledges that the play or theater is basically an illusion, and one can think of the main character, Prospero, as not only a magician but perhaps the creator of his own island—in other words, his plays. "Here Swims A Most Majestic Vision" comes out of *The Tempest* with two characters from that play. Miranda, who is the daughter of Prospero, and Caliban who is the half-man, half-fish freak of nature that used to rule the island that now belongs to Prospero. From owner of the island to becoming a slave to the new owner. In DeBoer's narrative, Caliban is a husband to Miranda, where their relationship devolves into a *Who's Afraid of Virginia Woolf?* style of nightmare. Drunk, depressed, and devoted to joyless sex, either with his wife, or a series of whores. Caliban is a figure of contempt with a side dish of pity. Like in Shakespeare's work, you know it is not going to end well. Yet, you the reader go through a journey mapped out by the author, and you learn how characters react under certain conditions. The original play can also be used to advance a new narrative, and like a jazz musician riffing off a popular song, DeBoer coaxes the Shakespearean language and narratives into his own story here.

The Two Gentlemen of Verona serves as the platform for the last story in this collection. "The Execution of the Sun" has only three characters: Valentine, Speed, and Julia. Shakespeare's *Two Gentlemen* is very much a screwball comedy of the Elizabethan Age (perhaps Shakespeare's first play), while DeBoer's reintegration has more of a dark tinge, with respect to love and following one's passion or sense of eros. "The Execution of the Sun" plays on the Greek legend of Phaeton, who chased the sun, and, of course, chose the wrong object matter to hunt down—yet, the glory is, that he lived for an intense moment or series of moments. Love can be that intense. But also, there is a need to be careful when one does catch one's desire—otherwise, it is sort of like the dog chasing the car. Again, the joy is in the hunt, but once desire is fulfilled, then life turns sour.

My admiration for *Annihilation Songs* is due to its playfulness with the text. I love language and textual play, and how a work from the past can translate into a new and totally original piece of literature. Jason DeBoer has the essence and talent to pluck history out of the shopping cart and onto the page, in a remarkable and unique style. In essence, the stories here are reflections or echoes of the original source, yet so different. Shakespeare and DeBoer share the same language, but what they do with it yields totally distinct results. DeBoer shows that he is inspired by the past, but more interested in using it to make something new. And out of the ashes of the Elizabethan Age, we have Annihilation Songs. Either out of respect for its source, or perhaps even revenge, this book, with DeBoer as its driver, is very much a superb ride. I'm very happy to sit in the side-car for this particular literary adventure.

Tosh Berman
—Author of *Sparks-Tastic: Twenty-One Nights with Sparks in London*

AUTHOR'S NOTE

This work is an experiment in which each and every word used in each story also appears in a particular William Shakespeare play, barring some modification of the original elision. The words of each play have been individually restructured into a new narrative. In effect, the language of Shakespeare has been fragmented and then reintegrated.

"Puzzles of War" was derived from *Hamlet*.

"Here Swims a Most Majestic Vision" was derived from *The Tempest*.

"The Execution of the Sun" was derived from *The Two Gentlemen of Verona*.

PUZZLES OF WAR

The assault on Normandy was over. Birds scratched curiously at bodies, the many shapes in the waves, and dark blood stirred the sea, turbulent and muddy against the fortified cliff. France was in ruin, a nation of graves and dead boys. Beneath the low battlements, Private Cornelius turned up the dirt with his pick-axe, where he and several rear guard privates were working as grave-diggers, packing friends and enemies into the same loathsome hole. "Dig deep because of dogs," a passing captain said, and the men did. The Norman sun made the dead bloat and split open, and like fat puppets with their strings cut, they fell drooping into the earth.

In the afternoon, a soldier hit a mine with a shovel, blasting him into the crow-flowers. He clawed at the dust, croaking red bubbles, as they picked shards from his throat. After a while, the privates and the doctor put him quietly in the hole. Husbands, nephews, and sons all fell mute beneath the spade. Cornelius dug until dizzy, his arms weeping dirty sweat. He looked up. A new ship was in the water, boarded by a stream of wounded in white rags. England's broken soldiers were already going home. Cornelius, woundless, watched each cataplasm enviously.

A canopy of metal angels made their flights from England, dropping death on the German lines, and the blasted earth shook like a kettle-drum clapped by a million angry hands. Breathing heavily, Cornelius had to wince at the flashes and clamour, and the distant violence seemed worse to him than the gore at his feet. He became unnerved and the first cracks appeared in his bravery. On break, he sat aloof from the others and read a pocket book about Nero. As Cornelius pulled cold food from a can, the immortal moon, still skyish as a pale morning apparition, fed his lunacy and seemed to say, "I will outlive all, even this rotten continent and its war."

Nero, that imperial changeling, ruled with the cool assurance of a distant star. Indeed, the weight of his crimes seemed to impress its horrible stamp on all of ancient history. Rome, that mother of monsters, actively esteemed the wild flourishes of his villanies, even though the vast millions of his empire dreaded his name.

The German army fell back, but their cannons still cleft the morn. A battery to the east had Cornelius and the Second Army in its range. The fight spread in all directions. In vain, England's armour battalions advanced and tried to cause havoc, but the stronger German armour repulsed them and held firm. The constant air strikes kept at some southerly target, and on occasion the silvered wings would be hit by ground fire and dip like flaming kites to their doom.

They buried soldiers in white sheets without ceremony or epitaph. The graves were not even permanent––after a month, the bodies would be dug up again and shipped to grizzled churchyards or proper grass-green plots. Sick to his stomach, with a blister on every finger, Cornelius could no longer endure the whiff of death, the dry loam in his eyes. His mind was steeped in funeral day dreams, fears of being swallowed by the ground. In desperation, he walked up to the sergeant for help. "No more, sir. No more. The flies, the smell…It's bloody hell, sir."

In a rage, Sergeant Laertes turned and cursed him. "What did you say, Private?"

"I'm losing my head, sir."

Laertes knocked him down with one hand.

"Sword Command says we need graves, Private. You will dig––*dig*, I say—until their order changes!" he said tyrannically, and whipped the men with more threats.

They started to dig again, but Cornelius moved stiffly, slow with insolence. That was it. He was through with duty. Hereafter, his only allegiance was to his sanity.

"Damn it, Private. Work!" The huge sergeant seized Cornelius roughly and shook him.

The private swore under his breath, but Laertes would not unhand his shoulder. Cornelius struck wildly and his pick-axe hit the sergeant in the skull. The two other privates, speechless, jaws open, scanned the scene. The hush was murderous. The company tyrant was now just a barefaced object bleeding in the dust.

"You'll hang," one said softly to Cornelius. The other tried to cross himself. They had despised the sergeant too, but were unbraced for his murder. "Run, Cornelius, you bastard." They frowned and gave him a push. "Run, you fool!"

It was a strange moment of friendship. In amazement, Cornelius looked at the body and met the force of his traitorous act. Fighting tears, he turned toward the forest and broke into a run.

His tutor Seneca had tried to teach the young Nero philosophy and justice, to make of him a new Julius

Caesar. But the youth was more intent on reckless pranks and lewdness. He was ashamed of nothing. Over time, Nero lost himself in incestuous bonds and even bedded his evil mother. Weary of his abuses, with his bites on her breast, she constantly forged plots to usurp him. In the end, he dispatched her to hell, just as he did Seneca.

Cornelius kept running, running, his lungs clambering up to the light. Back behind him, he heard a warning shot, then an alarm of loud cries. He thought of prison. Death. Yes, it would be death. They killed cowards because they were contagious. He picked up speed until the murder and its consequence seemed far behind.

Rome, a city fed on disasters, was in flames for seven nights, and its people roasted like fish in the streets. Craven and safe in his towering marble, Nero became strangely charitable and opened his huge garden to the city. Praying, they hid in the green from the hellish lick of light. Soon after, however, Nero received blame for the fire…

After a time, Cornelius found a small hamlet

that had been razed by air fire. Only the chapel still stood, cracked open like an egg-shell, and Cornelius heard a female voice within. Fearful, he tried carefully to creep unwatched into the chamber. The church was being used for a livery, full of animals, straw, and excrements. An old, wretched horse bent down to feed from a basket. The wrinkled priest lay blown asunder in the corner and his brains stained the gold cross on the wall. A pregnant girl sat on her knees, kissing a man. Her dead lover was a monstrous brute, his guts spread like adders across the straw. She would pinch his cheek and chide him in shrill-sounding French as she held his hand, tears crawling down the neck of her shirt. Cornelius made an accidental noise and the vacancy left her eyes, if only for a moment, as she turned to watch him in the shadows.

Feeling a blush, Cornelius pronounced his French dreadfully, saying he was sorry for intruding. She said nothing, but offered him some old bread. In the meantime, she kept up her whisper to the dead man, whose face bore a permanent yawn. Cornelius had a drink of foul wine, then asked her name. Gertrude told him. He gave her some money, a pound "for the baby," and she became less guarded, divulging her story in swift currents of speech. Her husband was ill, she said, from bad water. She always used the present to speak of him, as if his blood in her hair were just a dream.

It grew dark, but they did not build a fire for fear of air strikes. Gertrude gave Cornelius a blanket and made him a bed in the corner near the pile of the priest. From the split roof, the brazen light of the moon came in and smeared their bodies sugar white. He could not see her eyes, just the black likeness of a skull, as her ripe, milky form left him and returned to the straw.

When Gertrude thought she and her husband were alone, she removed her clothes and, in carnal glimpses, Cornelius saw her skin touch the cold, drooping face. Her lover beneath her, Gertrude groped at his death. Wearing a glassy expression, she sucked at his withered places, which would never rise again. She was a repugnant beauty pulled by lawless desires. Full of moan and vile grace. Aroused by the raw scent of the priest, Cornelius moved slightly to better peep at her hideous gestures.

"Gertrude," he said once in a whisper, incensed, then fell asleep and made love to her in his dreams.

The horrors of his rule made sure that Nero was feared. He held extravagant public events, where the Roman rabble were witness to fierce entertainment. Boisterous fighting, pomp clad in steel, whips. Calamity on earth. Dragged from mildewed dungeons, Christians were painted with offal and beaten, others quartered or poisoned with arrows. Spectators wagered on the dying men and beasts, as the Emperor cheerfully played host to it all.

Morning could not dispatch the heavy sadness from his heart, as if Cornelius were still corrupted from the night's events. The everlasting war had laid waste even to love, making it seem unnatural and dismal, a weak feeling fit only for peace. Awake and no longer naked, the girl looked distant. Distracted. Empty of desire. When Cornelius called her name, she appeared to mouth a quick confession to the priest, but then started smiling like a serpent and held a box to Cornelius in her open hands.

Her prize was venom. Gertrude had whored herself for liquor and army drugs. Already addicted to forgetting, she put a vial of Lethe in her arm and spent the morning in dull ecstasy. Cornelius copied her perdition, but it did not cure him of thoughts of Laertes, his eyes open, flat on the dirt, arms outstretched with a pick-axe for his crown. Cornelius told himself that it had been an act of war, a small affront to a desperate, guilty world. In the arithmetic of murder, what was one more? Sergeant Laertes was no saint, to be sure. There might not be a stern judgment by the army, Cornelius thought. Perhaps he would see home again. Drunk, his mind in tatters, he acted the fool and told Gertrude all about England and justice and liberty and his new life of leisure, but she did not understand a word.

Despite his reputation, Nero became something of a clown for his ostentation and low habits. He often appeared in a common theatre to ply the city with artless songs. Imperial guards would not allow the audience to leave, so they would applaud his weak voice in fear of his wrath. However, a few brave souls went so far as to play dead, in order to be removed from the tediousness of the performance.

After the drugs wore off, Cornelius grew angry with himself for these flashes of madness. He devised to take his chances behind the German lines, where he would be considered a prisoner of war and not a murderer. For, without a doubt, he was damned if he returned to his company. When he saw that Gertrude was dead or sleeping on her husband's shoulder, Cornelius stole the horse and quietly left the church. On his way out, he set the Nero book on top of the priest.

Smelling revolution, Nero made his escape from Rome. He fretted for his life in a farm house until the rebels caught him. Guarded only by a servant (who had been asked by Nero to kill himself so the Emperor could see how it was done), they found Nero in the middle of self-slaughter with a dagger in his neck.

Fat from luxury, remorseless, he died profanely like some diseased satyr in fancy garments. His god-like lunacies came to an end.

On horseback, Cornelius moved freely, without caution, even though he knew there was combat all about. The air and shine made him feel invulnerable. The forest was unshaped colour. Violets sharked through curls of grass, roses steeped their leaves in sickly green light, and thick perfume was in the wind, the ominous rot of flowers. Caught in the branches of a knotted plum-tree, a thin pastoral gallows, the limbs of an air borne soldier dragged in space like shameful fruit. Near Cornelius, a sparrow soiled the day with its tender song. He heard men up the trail.

In a slow line, a Free French convoy jangled down the country path. An engineer dismantled mines in front of the lead armour, and several German soldiers lay at his feet, boys broken apart like puzzles that would never be put back together. To make sure they were dead, the engineer gave a hard kick to their sides. He was intent on his work and Cornelius could see the sinews move in his jaw.

Suddenly, a maimed German gave a groan and the old horse became afraid and went back on its heels, sending the hectic convoy to their weapons. All at once, they aimed their riotous metals. One of the crew may have uttered "Halt!" in French, but Cornelius heard nothing, so lost was he in the rhapsody of his fate.

The shell cut through him much more softly than he would have thought. Cornelius raised his hands to surrender. Another shell tickled his guts, one touched his ear. Calmly, he hoped with all his might that he would not be buried, that the ground would not take him. He did not want the dirty sheet, the hole, the hallowed words. Thinking of ancient Rome, Cornelius fell and went black to his core, while the ulcerous sun kept burning the blue.

He got his wish for thirty hours, until the shadow of the first shovel appeared.

HERE SWIMS A MOST MAJESTIC VISION

Caliban was not the first to drown at home on the couch. He never died, no matter how much he should have. He only drowned. Slowly, instinctively. Here death did not work very hard. At night he lay there brained by his bottle of rye, solemn and patient like brown water, in repose as the moon graced midnight freckled with its own filth. The silence pleased Caliban. "Together, my bottle and me," he would whisper, alone, as if it were the only goodness.

It was a rotten carcass of a marriage and they both knew it. Still, there was a part that Miranda resolved to hold close, to restore and strengthen. It was a foolish wish. Madness. In his deafness, her project would die.

"It is only a falsehood that my remembrance summons," her conscience told her, but she did not understand.

Often, she thought it was no rift between them, but a coil of closeness, an irreparable discord in which the hurt was tended between them as some fertile indulgence. As if each were cruelly dedicated to the other...

She found a picture of them as a young barefoot couple, when his crimes were only "mischiefs." A time of ignorant comfort, when he bedded only her and they laughed with assurance that there would be no ending to their love.

"Hell is what my trust was then, as if I demanded to be wrong."

He had charmed her once, there *had* been gentleness, before the wilt of ardour. When did this sorrow supplant love? Their marriage was now an abysm and all her service slavery, the words *I love you* but a spoken vanity. The ensuing remorse made her ache. She suffered useless, human pains.

Miranda knew a little peace each day when Caliban was at work. She too found compassion in his rye and by the sixth glass she felt uplifted, severed from the apparition of her life. As the fumes killed her senses, she would embrace the table, perfumed with sloth. Lost. Forgetting for a while the sun's slow burn on the earth. Drunk. Stray grief dancing in her head.

"I long for the night, when even my blame sleeps."

No noises of children were in their house. She chose to be barren.

"I want no son, no father, no man any more."

Her lie to Caliban was that she came from a long line of bad wombs. A "hereditary defect." Caliban did not want to be a parent either. Still, he would mock her for the birth she could not, would not give.

All his credit was plunged into whores. Thousands lost in bondage and liquor. When he cheated in green and silver it disturbed Miranda the most, as these were the colours of the distance between them. She loved to molest a dollar, just as he lived to stroke leather black as pitch, and if she could not halt the drift of his love, she would fight for his money. To prevent or manage its loss, Miranda was inclined to a lingering vigilance, an inquisition each time he returned home. Austerely, with trials of cutting questions, she measured how much money was washing away. She would feed him guilt for dinner. It did no good. No amends came before her. None.

The liquor made her stronger and gave her confidence. At times she was insolent enough to roar at his waste, but in the end he had her bawling. Then he would leave to drink with the rabble, the dregs of his friends, to whistle at women and worse. Miranda had a vision of his unseen actions.

"All the devils with glasses raised, devouring any thing to try to fill their husks."

The scene crept distinctly into her imagination. Caliban, a drunkard without discretion. Mouth foaming to suck the breasts of a whore…

Waking from a noise, her dream was dismissed. She felt a swift dulling of hope. His approach always sounded the same. An odious footfall. Caliban would sway into the screen, fooling with his key, tripping on the step. Miranda was fearful. He entered the room, stooping for his bottle under the bed. He cursed and expelled a belch, stripping off his garments, and she thought fright might devour her. Danger swallowed the complexion from her face. But then nothing. He fell asleep. It was a good night when slumber hushed the enemy.

"Even his snoring is poisonous. It has the savour of ridiculous crimes."

Next to them lived a minister and his wife, both lightning white with the fear of god. Shrieking burst from their house every night at six. Caliban would turn off the news and stand observing through the glass. The minister, humming to his abominable heaven, beat his wife soundly yet preciously, as one would wreck a jewel. Their library shed its rattling din, lamps and holy books painted amply in blood and faith. He would crack her skull and leave her in a pile, then pray with a sanctimonious air, as if to wipe out his sin. His deity would remain mute and without miracle.

Caliban would spy on them, drink in hand, and learn. To him the spectacle was more than a beating, it was something gallant and dreadful, a strange prerogative of marriage.

"Light is the paragon of unworthiness, composed of an insubstantial god. Only darkness bears the hush of lasting power. Only darkness is without witness."

Caliban would then peer at Miranda through his empty glass. Her features melted and exposed only the wound of her mouth, a red circle fringed with teeth. She was a frail woman, a body, a standing displeasure.

Her mind and its prattle were even uglier to him,

and he told his bottle softly, "Within her chatter dwell all her stale qualities, but when silent she seems even louder at her lying."

His whores told him no lies. With them there were never any dull accidents of discourse. And no mouths could be as lush. His lust curled awake when he thought of them, skins malignant and divine, flat on their backs only for him. Deformed nymphs, hollow and unsettled on the bed.

"A twenty, my dear, to buy your poor, wet blemish..."

All the trash and entrails that his cock had swum through. All those hours of flesh and folly had become his dearest perdition. Shapes drenched in villanous sweat. Time bereft both of speaking *and* the desolate lack of speech. Caliban grew to cherish this blasphemy, this earthly desire to violate angels.

"Such evil can be wondrous... Come, my rotten one, bare your blemish and feel the disease in your veins. Abjure a prayer with me. Let us strive to rend this globe from its trifling heavens…"

He had need of these savage revels, to fuel the infirmity within him, to defy reason with something much stronger: the disgrace of the infinite. Each monstrous union, each lusty pinch in the dark, each gorgeous face he marred with his touch, each bashful virgin made to kneel and lick... Each one of these actions made a sovereign gesture that went beyond the edge of language and removed even the knowledge of death. His hope was that his rage, at its zenith, would threaten the world and its beginning, like flame held to straw. To invert innocence and poison time with ecstasy, to incite a mortal destiny yet repulse all thought of ends, to hiss at death as its power abates... Yes, it was the noblest celestial dare, to strike a blow against death. The impossible was at stake. If he cursed and struck it enough, would death itself perish? Caliban thought of these things and the condition of his prick.

He came home from the office, lost in grumblings till the bottle gave its kiss. He saw Miranda moping against the wall. She held the curtains and wept from the scarcity of love. The wetting of her eyes was her gift to him. A prize he could bear. An overblown compensation for the charity of his torments. Caliban often came home only to quarrel, to exercise his baseness and keep their marriage a perpetual wrangle. His need to torment her demanded it. His grudge against her had its own arms and head and beating heart, its own life.

Caliban took a drink and hunted for his fury. He came towards Miranda, strutting his malice.

"Come here, I'll make a maze of your teeth."

The threats far from idle.

"My princess of darkness, let me crown your precious skull."

After each loud aspersion, her nose curled deeper into her bosom. Caliban saw her as harmless and blind, a damned worm incapable of indignation. A lazy slave unfit to pour his drinks. He felt the disdain that only marriage can produce. Miranda kept silent, infused with a cramp of dismay.

"Trembling yields its answer," her misery spoke as she kneeled, delicate before the blows.

Given a bloody cheek, she was perfected. Peerless in her indignity and subdued for their unwholesome sex. He never made love to her, he infected her. She sadly presented him her behind, crying through brave, humble eyes.

"His cock begins to swell…and then…then the afflictions come," she thought before the groans.

His heaviness itself was terrible. Mounting her despair, he plunged all their enmity into her plain body, driving into its miserable obedience. When she was obedient, she held the most power over him. A tyrant lived in her bush then, which Caliban resolved to murder. He abhorred the manacle of her sex, the soft regions that had once stolen his love, that had made him worship then marry her. For years, his prick had been in a snare. The bachelor had been confined to the prison of a wife. Yet, those affections, that stale need for a companion, did not plague him any longer. The horrible time of loving

38

was over. A ghastly memory. His life was now a search for an abundance of pleasure, a lust without limit, where consciences would dissolve into the play of the senses, usurping temporal confines and bidding farewell to death. Painfully bound together in wanton sex, her fear kept nibbling at his weakness.

Blood, in unstanched drops, like wine made from her dead virtue, gave tribute to him. Her virtue, unnatural as a funeral to Caliban, was always invisible till it was stained. His hands imprisoned her waist, still shaking with dread and something else…contentious waves without precedent.

From her escaped a sudden word, "Monster!"

Her bare body flamed, treacherous. He seized angry breasts and felt in her the momentary vigour of a traitor. Amazement, fever transported him, and he grew frantic with passion. Wild. Incensed. Faster, he thrust into her, sighing at the strain of his discharge.

After, she lay alone, her back gilded with his ooze. Her eyes mudded with tears, the dew of mourning, and she brushed the blood from her saffron hair. Miranda then felt her hate like roaring winds, for Caliban, for herself.

"Forgiveness, no. Never. Never."

Full of drinks and a new fortitude, Miranda made a vow to pierce the paunch of his cunning. She plotted, a conspiracy of one, while he was out cradled in the laps of whores, sowing his evil. She *would not* be cheated of her revenge. Her being grew perfidious, a glut of pure treason.

The next night, Caliban left the house and, after a few hours, a fiend came home bearing his laugh. Wicked, full of drunken harshness, his suit stinking of sex, he drenched her in abuse. A vile rain of words. But his stinging tongue could not penetrate the thick fabric of her anger. Her very heart was howling for its freedom. Caliban stopped when he saw something mutinous in her stare. Miranda the coward had become proud and strange.

"Shut up, Caliban, you bastard."

She had the gallows in her voice, yet he quickly flung her aside. He would tame her mighty desperation.

"I'll kill you," he said and landed a blow upon her frown.

Miranda did not run. She moved to scrape his eyes with her nails. Tumbling together, they fell to the couch, throats hanging with fingers, and destroyed each other in quiet nuptial assaults. She was the weaker, and her arms soon fell in a droop. His bulk would not yield. The motion of his shadow, dropping like a dead god, had driven the breath from her. His teeth were bare with delight, as if he were playing a sport. Drunkenly, with a faint laugh, vows issued from him.

"I take thee as my wife... to hate, dishonour, and disobey. Yes, I do. I do. Marry me again, Miranda."

Caliban did not release her neck and her eyelids felt

a growing drowsiness, like a shroud. The closeness of the grave. She sucked the taste of bones. She *would* be cheated of her revenge. Her shaking hands hurried to find a weapon, hid with patience for this occasion. There. Under the couch. Something sharp. Swiftly, she raised its silver point. Caliban had no time to disarm her and could not deny her vengeance. Miranda saw his smile vanish.

The knife fell deep into one of his eyes, where the steel would remain. He stood upright to pluck the metal from its wound, and for a second his face held the dignity and noble shape of unicorns. She beheld the princely arch of his sinews. A surge of his pulse summoned up a royal plume of blood. Caliban felt the strange wink of one eyeball. Half blind, he could not remove the knife.

Bellowing, Caliban struck wildly at Miranda, bending to mark her with the secret of his new majesty. He lost his footing with a weak departing sound.

"Thus does sovereignty plummet…unwillingly."

Reeling, he fell away. She eyed the ebbing of his throes until his swim wearied to drown. Miranda felt a momentary envy as she beheld her loss. Doubt heaved in her stomach and her relief felt troubled. Oddly unrewarded.

"The disturbed tears of widows should be missing."

They were not.

The rite had ended. Her trembling nostrils moved as if speaking their own harmless language.

THE EXECUTION OF THE SUN

Time was eating his youth, so with little more than a nod, Speed parted from his wife. Slender, forlorn, fingering her gold ring. The train moved forward impatiently, ignorant of loss. Travel vanquished their marriage like so many before. There was engine noise. A whirlwind. The departure of faces. The wife suffered away, a jewel worth nothing. Sullen and undone at the window, Speed tried to weep, but his eyes were dully dry. Heavy with shame. Sleep, a remorseful drift inward, delivered him from the day, and the night descended as a slow, twinkling death.

Morning seized open. The sky came out naked

and unwelcome. Deeply uncertain of his journey, Speed tried to nurse his fears with liquor and talk. A breakfast of vices. The other passengers, a sea of couples, read the disgrace on his cheeks and soon shunned him as a traitor to love. Closest to him were a dignified man and a girl of about twenty. A proud waxen figure and a fresh young ornament, a companion with the stature of a mistress and not a daughter. After hours of silent exile, Speed entreated the man for the time.

"Two o'clock."

"Thank you, sir. Your name?" Speed forced a friendly smile.

"Valentine."

"Not the publisher?"

"Precisely the publisher."

"Fantastic! I write…"

Valentine laughed bitterly. "I know. You have the mark."

His nose was like a spur and his face was bankrupt of blood.

"The mark?"

"Yes. Engraved on you. The ragged integrity. Well nourished on melancholy, of course. The false nobleness. I can tell that you wish for words of raging honey, but, in the end, the page abhors you."

Speed gingerly held his anger. "So, is that what writers are to you? Worthless pricks? Disloyal thoughts from a publisher, I would think."

Valentine laughed again, but less coldly.

"Very good! Some revolt! You might do well to press some of that hate into your ink, boy. There is good reason why ink is the blackest substance on earth. It is intended to extol the rewards of infamy."

"That must be why I am a stranger to print. Also, my name is Speed, not boy."

"So you think. Speed, this is Julia."

"How do you do?"

Julia gave a small nod and turned back to the window. In its frame, the wilderness stood free from the plagues of industry, and the train discovered western frontiers, wheels hammering the steel lines on the ground. The plain was fading behind in an endless jade. As the crystal murmur of a river made music with its weeds, there was a motion of geese, exquisite against the desolate sky.

The men spoke to each other for a while about art and letters, but it was the stubborn silence of Julia that especially beguiled Speed. Sad and disobedient, as if banished to be a witness, the girl observed them with an indifferent yet watchful eye. Her bare leg had the whiteness of milk. So pale it was some sweet deformity, so tender Speed felt he was bruising her with his gaze. The girl stayed without words and he thought her perhaps deaf and dumb, yet even her breath had a remnant of eloquence, as if hope had died there, wailing. Buried in her moist eyes were secrets, an unsounded perplexity, as well as some ruinous concord, like the essence of a dead puppy. A gentle and miserable solemnity. Her scalp shed a tangle of auburn whips, unstaid against the lean presence of her body.

As Speed regarded her, a sudden blush painted Julia's face and said more than her silence, speaking movingly to his glances. She seduced Speed then. He was determined to have her, to bite her hair and kiss her heels, to exchange groans and flood her with nectar, to clothe his cock in her being and pluck the sighs from her mouth. His mind held a million names for the sum of his desires.

Valentine had seen the treachery of these blushes and turned to Julia with scorn. Knowing that he was now a rival, Speed quickly looked away to hide his lascivious thoughts. Shame and fear, the horns of love, cut into his heart. He felt ashamed at this birth of feeling within him, which stabbed at the memory of his wife and the remission of their love. Speed despised this new passion, fearing a sequel of his broken marriage. Just then, through the glass, the verdure held an unruly horse trampling a flower, pale as paper and beautiful, a solitary lily loitering on the pasture.

"Let us dine," Valentine said and thrust a glove at the passengers. "Their babble stings my ears."

In the supper car, the three became more acquainted over liquor and were soon senseless as angels, which spurred a lively, if peevish, talk. The liquor masked but hardly mended the spite between the men, and the air coloured with trouble. Full of harsh words on every subject, Valentine's wit became injurious and rude towards the other two.

Losing his patience, Speed observed, "Your success has only made you bitter, but you seem not hard so much as desperate. And to think I admired you because of your reputation... My god."

"Your god, your god…Let me teach you about

your god. Let me remedy that schoolboy faith of yours and show you the perjury of heaven. This Christian malady has made man an intruder on this earth, wishing for the grave, jealous of the dead. You base Christian sheep have profaned the present with your tedious prayers, complaining that the earth is fodder for our contempt, worthy only of disdain. To you, the world is perceived as just one more cell in the unseen prison called heaven. Like all reasonless wretches, you desire discipline, a corrupted god to feed you torment. You are prisoners devoted to the whip and are quickly lost without it. Enemies of pleasure, you have fasted too long from reason, only to feast on pity. This holy plot of yours is always unjust, Speed, for it spurns life!"

"Old age has drawn you into dream. You are mad."

The publisher pretended to take offence.

"Correction, sir, I am not old! You are most unmannerly for a sheep."

After dinner, Valentine willingly enjoined the discourse towards the meaning of love, pulling at the strings that laced them together. To impress Julia, Speed gave his opinion and trusted that she would interpret it.

"I think love is best as a heavenly power carried by a stranger."

"Is that what you learned in your universities? Boy, you have the poets' cowardice when you speak."

"Then what is love?"

"Love is a ripe, worthless word…and friendship is but a mutual vexation."

"You are both wrong. Love is a silent villain," Julia said in a whisper, with a dangerous wink at Speed, "journeying to newer crimes."

Although pleased, Speed had no reply to these, her first words of the day. Brow knit with wrath, Valentine plotted revenge.

In a quick salute, the publisher brought up his glass and spoke with a counterfeit mirth, both peremptory and hateful, "To our threefold doom…"

He left and was soon asleep aboard the other car.

With Valentine away and lustily forgotten, longing chafed their heart-strings. Speed chased Julia to his bed chamber, where a hungry touch waxed into excess. Her white went wild and Speed was unrivalled until morn, when Valentine knocked with an imperious hand and said, "Good morning, deceitful lovers." His voice punished their forgetfulness and revenged their mutual favours. In a fury, the train cleft the root of a mountain. The engine tried to scale the tower, a nameless mount anchoring the world. The high stone steeple fostered its own winter, pinched with ice the colour of teeth. Crusts of snow crept over the shadowy forest, which wound in ink garlands over the rocks.

For some reason neither enraged nor humbled by the circumstance, Valentine had the smile of a hangman when the lovers came to the table. Reading the paper, he spoke with no apparent jealousy.

"What is wrong, Speed? You look ill enough to heave up your soul. Where is your love, your 'heavenly power,' now? Lost in the infancy of guilt?"

Speed composed himself before he spoke, "Although you repulse me, Valentine, I intended no ingratitude to you. Who can quell the onset of such passionate affairs? It may have been wrongful, but I feel somewhat blessed, as if it were destined to take place. These are no random knots in my heart. I think we love each other."

Julia said nothing to this and paid no mind to either of them.

"Is this a confession, boy? Save such a conceit for your truant god. I should tutor you in a lesson in power."

"You always speak as if I were a Christian, Valentine, but I am not. I do not believe."

"Yet you have recourse to words like 'blessed' and 'destined,' employed in every Christian anthem. You are like a linguist that does not believe in the tongue! Like most trusting fools, you are the perfect Christian, ignorant that you employ its practices and adore its spirit. Your faith is a general one and thus all the more dangerous."

"I may claim these faults, but they seem unworthy of the penitence you have resolved for me. Cruel-hearted judge, are you passing penance on me because I desire a soul?"

"Boy, your soul is a trifle, the legacy of a clownish god who could only fail at sovereignty. A dead king, a sovereign fraud, a petty god stuffed with pestilence, worshipped by those who rehearse death and forget life! Yes, this degenerate ancestry has quite a story... with the father, an invisible beast, hammering his immaculate wench, who then bore a bastard son, an adored figure of peace who has fostered nought but war. A lout reputed as a lord, who wandered deserts to brag to sheep. A shepherd of man, a treacherous saint who enforced the fealty of lambs, a messenger of a god who taught only the merit of chains, who taught men to aspire to be servants. He dazzled the illiterate with every silly proverb, that sour Jew! That slave to parable! That beggar on a nail! How quaintly did his foul blood soften the cross. It entertained the world for a time, that most vile of pageants. Many are still fawning over his death, frozen with grief until his return. Their minds are still affected by the charity of his lies, still yoked by falsehood after two thousand years. Vain idolatry. Creatures so starved for answers that they would pray to nothing!"

"And what should give meaning to the life of man? His doubt? You give such import to slander, Valentine. Would you cancel all the triumphs of man and his god?"

"I desire man to exceed himself, but he esteems only safe, illumined thoughts. If man need worship an old past lost in dust, why not worship, say, Phaeton? Daring to endanger the world, he resolved to lawlessly tame the sun. Mad, mad Phaeton who died in true glory as he parted from transgression and descended in a coil of fire, unheedful of the possible, tempted by the most extreme sacrifice: the offering of the sun. If man offered up the sun, what a sacrifice that would be! If man would dare to penetrate the timeless and dispatch the infinite. To rend the sun and fly in its place would be the most valiant undertaking of all. Do you understand what that would signify, boy? No? Then I will convey it to you. And this earth—no, this train!—shall be the altar upon which we dispose of this celestial enemy. Once our grudge is appeased, we may then rejoice."

He took Speed and they crossed to the chamber of the publisher. Locked in with Valentine's possessions, a heap of clothes and money, Speed saw a rifle. Valentine took it and moved past Speed to a step ladder that gave access to an upper seal.

"The sun is but a sick pebble, the stars so much malignant dust. All those swoons of matter in their endless flight…I would wipe the sky of them all." He took the rifle and went up the ladder. "Come, boy, we will outrun idleness for awhile."

The wind came howling down the hole.

"Pure folly," said Speed, but an urge persuaded him to climb.

Valentine stood waiting on the far end of the car, indifferent to the rough motion of the train. Speed could not endure the reckless tilts and a stumble left him flat on his stomach. On his knees, he tried to creep near Valentine, who had the rifle aimed at the sun. The desert wound its golden scorn around them, hot frowns of sand enammelled with the shine of some deformed palace.

A whisper came from Valentine, "Here, even reason burns away. Killed by the light."

A shot took flight into the impossible, yet the wounded sun did not fall.

"Awful star, how many crimes will you commit? You spin there, flourishing yellow outrages at man, burning in your cloak of blood. Undeserving idol, you are not sacred! You have blinded man in so many ways, and, without eyes, we can only see god. Blindness has scoured us of reason. Unseeing, we seek truth in a fancy and love in a divine blot. You are a curse masked as a gift, and you wreathe the earth in dolour. I detest your deliberate, orderly lies! Your god is an absence, a trick of the light. See how you have hindered man with the error you conceal in your light. Enough! I'll have the day drowned in shadow."

"Valentine, only a fool hunts the sun. See, you flatter it with your volley."

"It is not flattery, but a censure."

The most unholy oaths came from him and the rifle kept blasting through the air into the monstrous mouth of fire, which graced its height as if patiently waiting to kindle every mortal thing. Great wings of dust washed down the train and away. Speed shut his eyes and closed his ears with his hands, wishing that the threats would cease. Despairing of the noise of the kill, he tried to plead for silence, yet his body could only shake.

It was not to be the swiftest execution, and the length of day could not quench Valentine's zeal as he railed against the object of his rage. After a period, Speed could hear Valentine wilt with a moan of thwarted vengeance. His face was a mask of meat and the rifle was out of shot. Still, he held his hands aloft and scratched at the light, as if to tear at the eyes of god.

Valentine chose to break the rifle in two and cast it away. He lay down with a sigh, "You are hers now, Speed. Go to your muse. You are a pawn and she needs that now. You are youthful and shallow and dull, and she needs that too. Love is feeble by nature, and I no longer care for it. For too many years, I have been an old emperor wringing beauty from a pearl. But treasure now gives me no delight. Beauty is now wearisome to me. I am enthralled by a new beloved: time. I would like to prove her necessity, Speed, yet I am unwilling to yield to the pillory of her form. I will woo death, homely as she is, but I will not wed her."

"I did not mean to steal Julia…"

"Should an heir talk of thievery? You have a boy's mind. It is she who will be robbing you…of your future. She has learned much from me. Go."

A fat, swarthy evening killed the sun contemptuously and without a word. With no light, the desert became only an embrace of shapeless heat. Weary and alone in repose upon the car, Valentine kissed perversely at the black air with his tongue.

The train stopped at the ocean with every cloud in grey turmoil. Water descended like tears without a head. Travellers charged the doors to disembark for the city, a huge urinal peopled with sorrow. Bold and crooked as a statue, the paragon of blackest judgment, Valentine overlooked the stream of hapless passengers.

"Come here, Speed, hear my last counsel." His mood suggested danger and conclusion. "This journey may vex you, but it is best that you are ignorant now. It will take time to understand your pilgrimage into vice. You promised Julia love, but she has no interest in it. She is your master, not your prize. You mistook her prodigious silence for a disability, but it was only a disguise concealing the hazard of her delights."

The advice angered Speed.

"Is this your cunning requital, Valentine? This talk of Julia? You waste your protestations."

"See, she has possessed you and made you her play thing. She will force you to your knees and govern your rashness for awhile, until you too are lacking all loyalty. For you see, Speed, we thrive only when we break bonds. Strength thrives in neglect not love. It is a vantage not derived from small pains. In you and in me, in Julia and even in your wife, there is a surfeit of broken vows, and in this adversity reigns our most conceitless pride. Some day, Julia will forsake you, but this banishment will temper you into one of us. It will dignify you and make you more worldly. You will inherit much from the exhibition of her hate, once you have refused the influence of love."

Valentine's voice became milder yet more earnest, "Even toys can become as lions, if they overtake the master who loathes them."

Then he vanished into the night and its pissing sky.

The wanton hooks of Julia's arms held Speed severely as she took him down the weeping street. The chameleon of a girl had now aged into an obdurate queen, and the cloister of her bosom disclosed the skill of its treachery. With an empress' grace and the sly voice of a wife, she spoke of duty. Marriage. She persuaded him to conspire with her, to bind each other to neglect as if it were some grievous form of wealth. Sufficient ransom for his pride. He would lose a fortune in love for the privilege of her company, but if he prevailed, it would be a bargain. Julia would fashion him into a man who would shrink from nothing. He had cherished the muse in her, but that soon died, melting like pills in the tide. Sadly drenched in his mistake, now betrothed to the unknown, Speed walked like a puppet or a hanged man.

He considered Valentine's inscrutable words and what they could mean. Already altered by his experience with Julia, he felt reformed into a lamentable state, yet some how bolder. Sojourned in his concern was the presence of a new integrity. In the wreck of his heart, he felt the fear again, but in stead of shame, an outlaw desire: the urge to ascend and mar the perfection of the sun.

POSTSCRIPT: KILLING THE DOGS OF KATHMANDU

1. The day is ours. / The bloody dog is dead.
—Shakespeare, *Richard III*

2. The creation of the first of these Shakespeare "reintegrations" began in 1996. I had entered Kathmandu in the midst of thieves. I knew so by the way they watched me and signaled each other. Three of them, a motley team of kids, maybe seventeen at most, had targeted me at the outer bus station. They didn't make their move then, but they positioned themselves, eyes serious and hungry, as we got on the first city bus.

The harrowing trip from the Indian border had worn on my nerves. A peasant girl unused to travel had sobbed and vomited for four hours, and on the uphill slopes, the liquid crawled back across the bus floor and kissed at my boots. Smoking cigarettes didn't dispel the stench, and the wall-to-wall passengers and the screaming radio and the aisles clogged with chickens and dusty sacks of grain beat at my senses until I didn't even care about the ever-present thousand-foot drop outside the window. It wasn't good to travel scared, and when exhaustion had crushed it out of me, I felt relieved, and as the lurching bus pondered suicide on every mountain curve, I felt no fear.

Getting to the ancient heart of Kathmandu from the outer station required three separate buses. Straining under my pack, I had to run like hell to catch the second bus and so did the thieves. One of them didn't make it. The bus was no more than a gutted van with plastic handles nailed to the ceiling, grasped desperately by twenty ragged travelers. I stood inches from the grin of one of the thieves. Each of us knew that the other knew, but the cat and mouse continued. I kept my backpack tight against the wall of the van, away from both thieves. I couldn't guess what they imagined I possessed of value. When the van stopped, I feigned relaxation, letting most of the passengers disembark ahead of me. The second thief lit a cigarette outside and was swept away by the crowd, while the smarter thief stuck close. I saw my break when the third van was nearly loaded to the brim. "Excuse me," I said to the nearest thief and then jumped out and sprinted to the third van as it closed its doors. The smart one stayed right on my ass, but the slower kid was pushed out by the ticket taker because the vehicle was overloaded. That left the one thief, who had stopped grinning.

Outside, I saw a young Nepalese mother in the doorway of her hut, clutching a screaming baby. The most beautiful woman I had ever seen in my life, despite her squalor and the strain on her face. The bus unloaded on the Durbar Marg, with the distant red temples of Durbar Square to the west, and the thief got out ahead to wait for me. Rather than let him tail me, I walked right up and shoved him to the ground. "Fuck off, you! Fuck right off!" India had made me mean. Flat on his back, his eyes flashed murder, but the open boulevard and surrounding crowd took away all his options. He swore in Nepali and scurried off. A pair of mangy street mutts began to sniff at my boots. I felt goddamn exhausted, but I was finally in Kathmandu, where I hoped to write and print my first book.

3. Mefloquine, an antimalarial drug often prescribed to travelers to malaria-infested areas such as India and the lowlands of Nepal, has these common side effects: insomnia, hallucinations, hair loss, insomnia, depression, psychotic dreams, unusual thoughts or behaviors, confusion, suicide, fatigue, seizures, insomnia, goddamn insomnia.

4. At one of Kathmandu's many book stalls, I traded in my copy of Balzac's *Droll Stories*, which I had read on the grass in the gardens in front of the Taj Mahal, a tiny oasis of peace and sanity amidst the chaos of India. I chose a collection of Chekhov stories and the complete Shakespeare for my next

reads. I took them back to the Hotel Utse, where in the lobby a diverse group of travelers had gathered to drink near the television, which always seemed to be playing the sixties *Batman* series. In addition to myself, there was: a German philanthropist named Hans, who paid money from his own pocket to send several Nepalese kids to college; a rugged Australian biologist, Marcus, who belonged to a tiger protection group; an obnoxious retired Greek, Christos, who loudly abused and badgered the hotel staff at every opportunity; Christos's tragic wife, name never divulged, who was the firsthand witness to his hundreds of daily bad behaviors; and Anand and Jagan, two middle-aged owners of a garment factory, who each evening had different call girls on their laps. We bonded each evening and became friends over beer and the local apple brandy and, on rare nights, hot toomba, the fermented millet tea served in tiny barrels with straws.

5. Mefloquine users should avoid drugs, alcohol, and especially toomba.

6. At night, I read the same pages of *The Tempest* over and over. I was too tired for it to take hold. I hadn't slept in two weeks. And not in the casual way one might complain of a restless night, a few missed hours, some tossing and turning. No, this was eyes open, humming brain, wanting to die insomnia. Insomnia underlined in red ink. For days and days on end. After two weeks, I actually thought I would die from it. I pondered what faxed message to send my girlfriend and future wife. The weakness, the letting go, crept into my bones. And in those closest moments, when sleep teased me and seemed to draw near, suddenly, the street dogs would explode into barking below my room. The stray dogs that slept all day in the sun, lazy and unafraid, clogging every entryway and nook in the Kathmandu alleys, came alive at night. Shakespeare's dogs of war. Fighting, fucking, howling, shrieking, but most of all attacking my exhausted brain. "Let me sleep, dogs of war! Cry havoc somewhere else…"

7. I have given a name to pain, and call it "dog".
    —Nietzsche, *The Gay Science*

8. I bought a knife. A long khukuri knife, the weapon of the famed Ghurka soldiers. They were sold everywhere in the city, and in the streets, hundreds of touts also sold a strange ointment called Tiger Balm. "Tiger bomb! Tiger bomb!" they'd shout in my face. Such a bomb is not very appealing when one is deathly tired. But a knife is to be treasured.

9. Exasperated with *The Tempest*, I realized I hated Shakespeare and I hated his dogs of war and any other fucking creatures that dared to make noise in the night. The idea came to me of disintegrating and then reintegrating Shakespeare's text into something new forms, so I took my knife and chopped up my copy of his play. My story "Here Swims a Most Majestic Vision" slowly took shape. And "slowly" is not an exaggeration. It's not an important fact, but I doubt many stories in the history of literature have been so painstakingly written. Literally constructed (or reintegrated) word by word and then meticulously cross-checked against the play, it took me more than two years to complete the final draft. But in Kathmandu,

the process was quicker, more brutal. A blade cutting up a text and rearranging the pieces. Paper substituting for the soft throats of loud dogs. I had always been an animal protector, a dog lover, but the insomnia had made me desperate and insane. For the sake of sleep, I vowed that the dogs below my window had to go. Otherwise, the sleeplessness would bury me.

10. We had an impromptu party on the hotel roof. A weird Indian businessman was reading people's fortunes from their faces. Mine was positive, even though I felt like a walking corpse already, but he told German Hans that someday he'd die in a car crash, which didn't help the festive mood. The Greek asshole was louder than the party, more grating than the dogs. My brain wanted him dead. The tiger biologist, Marcus, wasn't sleeping well either and after six beers each, I coaxed him to tell me why. His assignment as an environmentalist that day was to confront a shop known to deal illegally in tiger teeth and claws. He leaned in to whisper the rest. "We dragged the guy into his basement…" He paused and drank deeply, unsure

if he should continue. "And we beat him and beat him until he was just a fucking bloody mess." I had never heard of animal rights advocates waging thuggish war before. "Was he… alive?" "Sure, we're not murderers." His mournful face, his fortune to be read, tried to push the horror back behind the wall of alcohol. I could tell he wanted his statement to be true, but he had doubts. A boisterous man, usually, he now acted as if, in scrubbing the blood from his hands that day, something else had washed away too. We spent the next hour debating how his group could prioritize tiger lives over human ones, and his argument hinged on the rarity and beauty of the cats. "It matters that they survive. It fucking matters," he said. We smoked cigarettes solemnly and at some point noticed an aberration in the sky. "See that blurry star? It's in the same spot from hours ago, isn't it?" "I'll be damned. Even the stars are disintegrating." A ghostly comet flew above us and the Himalayas and I could feel my eyes water. The dogs seemed to react to the new object in the sky with even greater fury.

11. Every dog is valiant on his own dunghill.
    —Proverb

12. I spent the next morning roaming the streets and shops looking to buy poison. I even asked the tiger bomb salesmen if they knew where I could get some. Instead, I received suspicious glances and looks of pity, as if I were the world's most awkwardly incompetent murderer. I suppose I was. In the daylight, the street dogs snored peacefully, exhausted from their nightly antics. I went back to my room and finished the final carving of the pages of *The Tempest*. I wrote out a working concordance of Shakespeare's words that I most wanted to use in my reintegration. The "Here Swims a Most Majestic Vision" storyline had distilled into that of an abusive marriage with a wife rising up from her oppressor, and where the husband yearns to transcend death through his erotic deeds. It was an expansion on a minor theme of Sade's that had explored how the "little death" might defer the big death. Insomnia had made death feel very close, too close, so I tried to explore escape plans via writing. The cut-ups reflected my own inner fragmentation.

13. Jacques Lacan named one of his dogs Justine, after Sade's novel. Lacan also married Georges Bataille's ex-wife Sylvia, an actress most famous for Jean Renoir's film *Partie de campagne,* which has the most ironic cameo in cinema history, with atheist Bataille as a priest. Of course, in reality, most psychoanalytic sessions and days in the country have been ruined by barking dogs. No doubt, Lacan's most feckless patients were writers on mefloquine.

14. Just as I forced *The Tempest* through a process of disintegration and ended up with a reintegration called "Here Swims a Most Majestic Vision," so did my Kathmandu self dissolve from insomnia and morph into something stronger. One morning, the Greek saw me taking my meds and told me, "You do not need it in Kathmandu. No malaria." Within a few days, I could sleep again. Only then did I realize that my hell had been self-inflicted from the anti-malarials. I had been poisoning myself for no reason.

15. The dogs of war did not grow silent, no, but

their nightly noise no longer mattered. Elated, I even scratched their ears during the day and tossed them scraps. I needed pets, companions, even Shakespeare, to join me where I was going. I needed to move beyond the initial blasphemous thrill in taking a knife to the work of a luminary like the Bard. Severed from their contexts, the individual naked words had revealed to me how persistently violent and theoretically rich Shakespeare's vocabulary was and continues to be. Even the comedies have a darkness and complexity of idea that I never would have imagined before I began this project.

While constructing my stories, it became apparent how readily Shakespearean language assimilated with the ideas of controversial theorists like Friedrich Nietzsche, D.A.F. Sade, and Georges Bataille. The violence of Shakespeare's language in *The Tempest, The Two Gentlemen of Verona,* and *Hamlet* seemed to have many affinities with the atheistic, transgressive works of these philosophical thinkers. After Kathmandu, in these three reintegrations, I endeavored to explore themes that wed Shakespeare to more radical intellectual traditions. This work is still ongoing with the fourth reintegration in progress, "A Fallow Heart," which comes from *The Merry Wives of Windsor.*

Jason DeBoer is the founder of Trembling Sun Films. His feature film *Dead River* has garnered critical acclaim and awards in Europe and the United States. His writing has been featured in *The Iowa Review, Quarterly West, The Barcelona Review, Stand, Exquisite Corpse,* and other publications.

www.tremblingsun.com